Veritas

Through the Portal

BOOK 1

DANISH H.

Veritas: Through the Portal

Danish H.

Published by
Veritas Seeker Publications
www.veritasseekerpublications.com
info@veritasseekerpublications.com
ISBN - 978-1-7635725-4-6

CONTENTS

Worlds Apart: Loading...

In the near future, virtual worlds have evolved beyond screens and controllers, becoming fully immersive realities indistinguishable from life itself. Among them, one platform stands above all others: Sandcraft. Here, imagination reigns supreme; anything a user dreams becomes instantly tangible. Players enter Sandcraft through DreamCaps, advanced immersion pods that lull the body into a gentle sleep while the mind explores vivid, customizable landscapes.

Unlike life on Earth, SandCraft offers a world without limits. Want to build a towering castle? A snap of the fingers. Need a sparkling lake teeming with magical creatures? Simply picture it. It's a realm free of constraints, mistakes or frustrations; a perfect escape. Yet, perfection often brings emptiness. SandCraft provides instant gratification, but something deeper seems to be missing.

In the midst of this digital paradise, a new, unexpected phenomenon emerges: a mysterious stone archway. It appears unbidden within the endless landscapes of SandCraft, glowing with an enigmatic energy that suggests something far older, and far more real, than the world it resides in. Beyond the archway lies a realm known only by rumours: Veritas.

Veritas is not like any world created within SandCraft. It exists somewhere between illusion and reality, a place where true creativity thrives, but fulfillment is earned. Here, nothing is instant. Challenges arise, setbacks are frequent, and progress is hard earned. Unlike the carefully crafted perfection of SandCraft, Veritas offers a different kind of journey, one where the stakes are real, and the experience authentic.

But Veritas does not reveal its mysteries easily. It waits, patiently, watching, for those willing to seek out its truth.

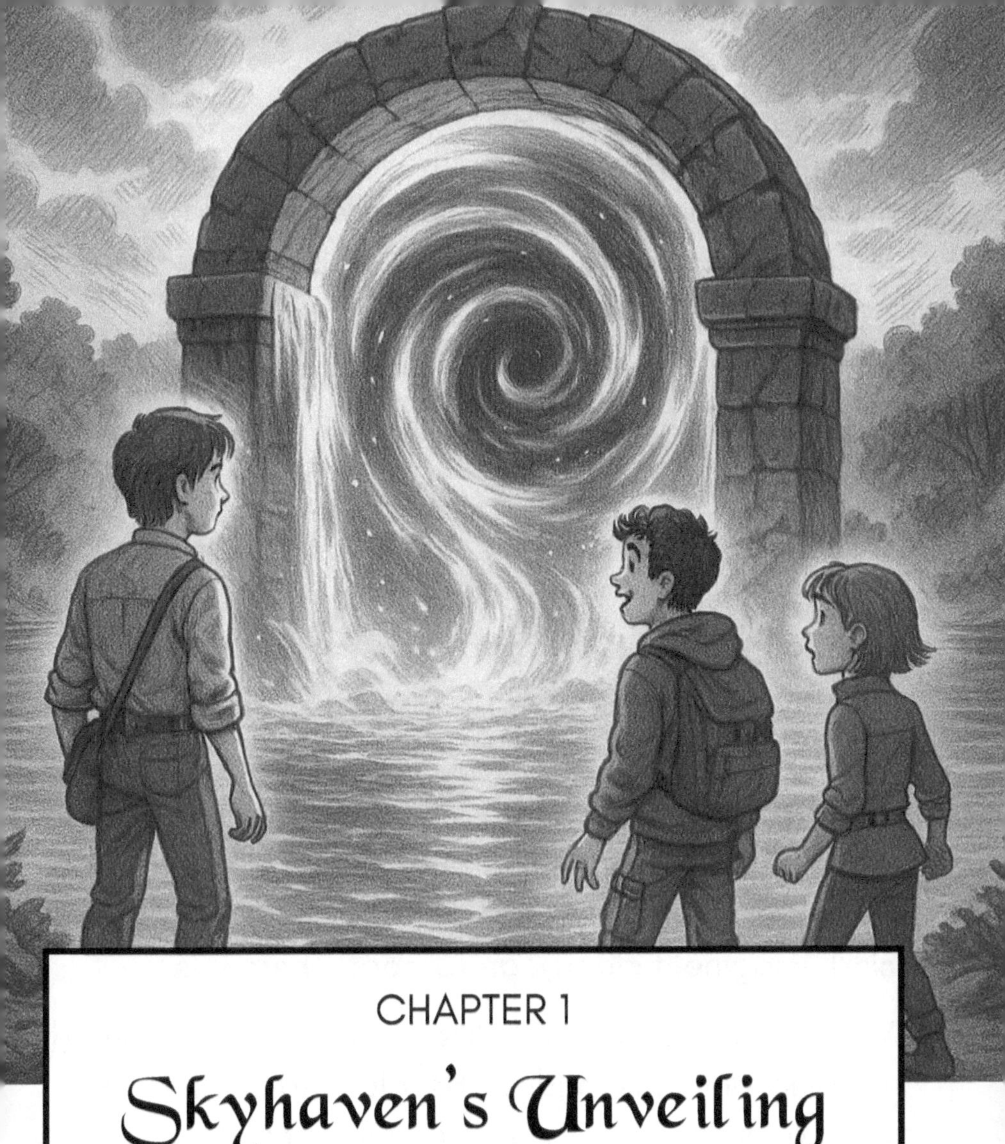

CHAPTER 1

Skyhaven's Unveiling

Sami stood at the shimmering edge of
Skyhaven's grand lake, its surface reflecting
twilight shades—violet, tangerine, and rose-pink. Tiny
sparks of light danced along the shore, an effect Sami

had meticulously crafted in SandCraft. Each tree around him had leaves shaped like emerald crystals, gently chiming with a musical whisper whenever a breeze blew.

He loved this world, his finest creation—yet even as pride warmed his chest, a nagging sliver of doubt crept in.

"Whoa... Sami, this is crazy," Jax breathed, brushing his hand against a glowing willow leaf. He was tall, with curly hair that refused to stay neat, and wide eyes that sparkled with amazement. "I've never seen anything this real in a virtual sandbox!"

"Thanks," Sami said, snapping his fingers. Instantly, a golden bridge arched gracefully across the lake, shimmering softly. "In SandCraft, it's all about your mind. Imagine it clearly, and... poof! There it is."

"Wish real life worked like that," Jax murmured, stepping onto the bridge. He glanced back at Sami with a sigh. "No waiting, no messing up—just perfection."

Sami began to agree, but the strange unease twisted inside him again. Something felt off, like spotting a blurry reflection in water.

A voice cut through the quiet twilight.

Mira stepped out from behind a crystalline oak, arms folded casually. "So, this is the famous Skyhaven? It's definitely... sparkly." Her tone hovered between impressed and skeptical—the kind that always got under Sami's skin.

Mira wore her short, dark hair pinned up with gears and bits—forever tinkering, building robots in her garage, or pulling apart old circuit boards. She never touched SandCraft, which made her stand out at school.

"You'd like it more if you gave it a shot," Sami replied, feeling slightly defensive. "No glitches. No frustration. Just perfection."

"Exactly," Mira said with a frown. "Too perfect. Where's the fun in that? Real building's messy—they have mistakes." She gestured at the sky. "Don't you ever wonder if you're missing out on real colors? Real sounds?"

Jax leaned thoughtfully on the bridge's railing. "But it's awesome, right? Floating islands, crystal trees, flying fish—stuff we'd never see back home."

"Sure, but is it real enough?" Mira challenged gently. "Aren't you bored with getting everything by just..." She snapped her fingers dramatically, imitating Sami. "Poof?"

Sami opened his mouth to argue, but the words tangled between pride and uncertainty. Before he could reply, a sudden rumble trembled beneath their feet. The peaceful lake stirred into ripples, waves splashing softly onto the crystal shore.

"What's that?" Alarm crept into Jax's voice.

The lake's center began to churn. Moments later, something rose from the water with a low hiss—a towering stone archway, ancient and dripping. At its heart swirled a glowing vortex of light, shimmering in colors Sami had never imagined.

"Sami... Did you—?" Jax started, but Sami quickly shook his head.

"No. I didn't build this."

Mira circled the shore cautiously, eyes wide with fascination. "Then how did it get here? SandCraft only makes what we code or imagine, right?"

A gentle pulse radiated from the portal, rhythmic and inviting. Sami moved closer, curiosity surging. He reached out and touched the swirling vortex. It felt warm—alive somehow. For a brief second, he thought he heard whispers like distant windchimes.

"Sami, careful!" Mira warned, gripping his sleeve.

"But what if..." Jax whispered, "it leads somewhere incredible?"

"Or dangerous," Mira added, though her own eyes glittered with cautious excitement.

Sami's pulse quickened. This was no ordinary sandbox glitch—it felt different, real in a way Skyhaven never could.

"We'll never know unless we try," he said softly, his heart racing. "Besides, we can always snap ourselves back out... right?"

Jax exhaled deeply. "Guess we'll find out soon."

Mira nodded reluctantly. "I can't believe I'm doing this..."

Hand in hand—Sami leading boldly, Jax steady at his side, Mira gripping Sami's arm—they stepped into the radiant portal. Light enveloped them, swirling endlessly in color and sensation.

"SandCraft or not," Sami whispered, "this feels more real than anything I've ever made."

And with that final thought, they vanished.

<u>Mira's Field Note 1</u>

Date: The day we found the archway. Still can't believe it appeared out of nowhere.

Location: "Skyhaven" (Sami's creation. but something else invaded it!

Observations:

- Arch made of unknown stone—surface glowed with odd runes.

- Vortex seemed warm to the touch. almost alive.

- Jax insisted we explore. I'm torn—my love for real adventures says "yes." but my gut says "this isn't normal."

Hypothesis:

If SandCraft only manifests content we design or code. this archway was definitely not coded by Sami. Maybe it's from the rumored "Veritas" realm I read about in those old e-zines. If so. the next steps could be...

dangerous.

CHAPTER 2

Through the Portal

Sami felt a thrilling rush the instant he stepped

through the archway—a bizarre mix of floating in warm water and plunging through open space. Colors whirled chaotically around him, and for a breathless moment, he wondered if he'd ever land. Then, suddenly, everything slowed, gently placing him onto solid ground.

Blinking to clear his vision, Sami stared in wonder. Massive, ancient trees stretched upward like pillars supporting a vaulted roof of intertwined branches. Sunlight pierced through gaps in the leaves, casting shimmering golden patches onto the soft moss beneath.

Jax stumbled forward, catching himself on a low branch. "Whoa," he whispered, voice shaky. "It's like we're inside a cathedral—but alive."

Mira knelt down, brushing her fingertips against the velvety moss. "This isn't normal sandbox stuff," she murmured, eyes wide. "The textures, the smells— they're...real."

Sami inhaled deeply, filling his lungs with a crisp, earthy scent. Gone was Skyhaven's flawless glitter—this world buzzed with genuine life and mystery he'd never imagined or coded.

"What if," he began quietly, "this place really is real?"

Mira's curiosity lit up. "You know, I read about something like this on old SandCraft forums. They called it Veritas, a place where everything has to be earned—not just imagined. I always thought it was a myth..."

A soft rustle drew their attention. A woman emerged gracefully from behind a wide tree, her silver hair woven into an elaborate braid. Her robe shimmered with patterns shifting gently with every movement.

"Welcome, travelers," she said, voice gentle but commanding. "I am Elara, one of the Secret Architects." Her kind gaze settled on Sami. "We've been expecting you."

Sami's heart raced. "Expecting us? But we just found that portal by accident."

Elara smiled warmly. "No discovery is ever truly accidental. We've watched your creations, Sami. Skyhaven was impressive, but as your imagination soared without limits, it began to lose its depth."

Jax spoke up quickly, defensive. "But Sami's the best builder in SandCraft. Everyone at our school says so."

Elara inclined her head gently. "His talent is unquestioned. Yet creativity is more than conjuring instant perfection. True depth comes from limitations—patience, challenge, even failure. Veritas was once humanity's greatest muse, now overshadowed by instant, easy virtual worlds."

A twinge of guilt tightened Sami's chest. Had he truly grown complacent? Was that why Skyhaven felt so oddly empty?

"What exactly are you saying?" Sami asked, feeling a bit defensive himself.

Elara stepped closer, warmth radiating from her presence. "I'm saying your imagination is extraordinary, Sami, but it lacks genuine struggle and growth. To rediscover your spark, you must journey deeper into Veritas."

She gestured toward a narrow path winding among giant roots and lush ferns. "You'll face real trials—tasks demanding effort and resilience. Only then can you restore balance to your creativity."

Sami squared his shoulders, remembering the hollowness he'd felt in Skyhaven. "I'll do it," he said firmly. "Show me the way."

Jax swallowed audibly. "I'm coming too. If it means seeing more of this place and learning something real." He sounded nervous but intrigued.

Mira smiled slightly, placing a reassuring hand on Sami's shoulder. "I never thought I'd say this about something half mythical, half virtual—but count me in. We tackle challenges together, right?"

Elara's eyes sparkled with approval. "Then follow me. The first step is always hardest, but trust yourselves—and each other."

She turned gracefully, guiding them deeper into the shadowy forest. As Sami, Mira, and Jax followed, their footsteps muffled by moss, a hush fell across the ancient trees. Sami's excitement mixed with uncertainty, like stepping onto a stage with no idea what role awaited him.

<u>Mira's Field Note 2</u>
Entry Title: "Arrival in Veritas"
Observations:

- Trees: Possibly centuries old. trunk circumference suggests enormous age. Leaves glow subtly in sunlight.

- Elara: A "Secret Architect"—her robes shimmer with shifting thread patterns. Could the threads be storing data or magic?

- Veritas: Feels alive—crisp air. real smells. gravity slightly different? Hard to say. My skin tingles.

Side Thoughts:

- Jax seems nervous. Is it fear of unknown? Or worry about failing in a realm that doesn't guarantee instant success?
- Sami is both excited and defensive—he might be worried Veritas will reveal he's not as unstoppable as he thought.
- I should keep my eyes open: who knows what else roams this forest?

CHAPTER 3

Trials of Creativity

Agentle breeze sifted through the towering trees, carrying the distant scent of wildflowers and damp earth. Sami, Mira, and Jax followed Elara along a winding path that led into a secluded clearing, its edges framed by twisting vines studded with glowing buds.

Elara paused at an archway formed from roots and luminous orchids. "Your first trial lies beyond," she said, gesturing calmly. Through the arch, the trio could see partially built bridges, incomplete sculptures, and half-constructed towers—each abandoned before it was finished.

Jax drew a sharp breath, eyes darting from one unfinished project to another. "What *happened* here?" he whispered.

Elara laid a gentle hand on one of the half-carved statues. "Long ago, many came to Veritas hoping to create magnificent works. But when the tasks grew difficult, they gave up. These structures reflect their lost patience."

Sami felt a pang of recognition, recalling how quickly he'd conjured entire worlds in SandCraft. No struggle. No real progress.

Mira frowned, tapping a partially built mechanical contraption that looked like it was meant to move but lay rusted and neglected. "So... our job is to finish what they started?"

Elara nodded. "Yes. Patience and sustained effort are the keys here. You must learn that true creativity often requires frustration, setbacks, and perseverance."

Sami exchanged a look with Jax and Mira, then stepped under the archway. The moment they passed through, Elara disappeared behind them in a swirl of faint light, leaving the three alone with the tasks ahead.

The Creations of Patience

Scattered across the clearing were three major projects, each in different stages of abandonment:

1. A Phoenix Statue: Stone feathers half-carved, lying in piles of chipped rock.

2. A Collapsing Bridge: Gaps in its supports, timbers cracked and misaligned.

3. A Spiral Tower: The base nearly complete, but the middle floors half-finished, rubble strewn about.

The Phoenix Statue

Mira walked up to the phoenix sculpture, running her fingers along its rough, unfinished wings. "Whoever started this had real talent," she murmured, admiring the careful details of the creature's eyes and beak. "But it looks like they stopped once the wings got complicated."

With a gentle sigh, she pulled a small chisel from her belt pouch—one of many gadgets and tools she always carried.

"I can try to shape these feathers, but it'll take time. And... I've never done stone carving before."

"You've got this," Sami encouraged. "Just remember what Elara said—keep going, even if it's slow."

The Bridge

Jax stood in front of the precarious bridge, brow knitted in concern. "It's... so unstable. If I fix one support, another might slip." He glanced back at Sami, worry etched across his face. "What if I mess it up more?"

Sami offered him a reassuring grin. "We can double-check each board together. I'll help haul materials, or hold beams in place."

But Jax swallowed hard, recalling all the times in SandCraft where a quick fix was just a click away. "Okay," he said softly, voice trembling, "I'll try."

The Spiral Tower

Finally, Sami approached the partially collapsed spiral tower. Loose stones lay in heaps. He knelt to pick one up—it felt surprisingly heavy and cool against his skin. In SandCraft, a tower this tall would've taken him mere seconds to conjure. Yet here, every stone had to be chosen, lifted, fitted carefully. Part of him cringed at the sheer amount of manual effort.

"No shortcuts," he reminded himself under his breath.

Hard-Earned Progress

For the next few hours, the clearing resounded with the scrape of chisel, the creak of timbers, and the clack of stone as the three friends tackled their tasks:

- Mira painstakingly carved feather after feather on the phoenix's wings, discovering her knack for detail-oriented work. Whenever she felt frustrated, she'd pause, examine her progress, and try again.

- Jax, shaky at first, gradually gained confidence in bracing planks and measuring each beam's placement. He discovered that the repetitive nature of hammering nails and testing supports could feel oddly calming, once he allowed himself to slow down.

- Sami kept rebuilding the tower's middle section. Each stone required deciding the best fit, angle, and stability. Sweat dripped down his forehead, but instead of annoyance, he felt satisfaction every time a piece slid perfectly into place.

"I never had to focus like this in SandCraft," he thought. "But I kind of...like it."

Every so often, he'd glance over to see Mira beaming at her slowly forming phoenix sculpture, or Jax stepping back to admire how the bridge was—miraculously—still standing. Their small victories fueled his own determination.

The Completion

Night fell, but the clearing remained lit by vermilion glowing flowers twined around the vines, providing a soft, magical radiance. Finally:

- The phoenix stood tall, wings unfurled in graceful arcs, each feather etched with painstaking detail.

- The once-wobbly bridge now formed a sturdy path across a small ravine, no longer threatening to snap beneath a single step.

- Sami's spiral tower rose skyward, each block carefully set. A gentle golden glow began emanating from the base, as if the tower itself recognized their achievement.

Elara appeared at the edge of the clearing, a proud look in her eyes.

"Well done," she said, voice soft yet brimming with approval. "You have taken the first steps toward mastering true creativity."

Mira pressed a hand to her sweaty brow, a tired grin stretching across her face. "That was...hard," she admitted. "But...worth it."

Jax couldn't stop staring at the repaired bridge. "I've never felt more proud of something I actually did with my own hands," he said quietly.

Sami exhaled, heart pounding from both exhaustion and excitement. "I never knew how...fulfilling it could be to work *this* way," he confessed. "Real effort, real mistakes, real progress."

Elara approached, resting a reassuring hand on his shoulder. "Never forget this feeling. It is the foundation of authentic growth. Patience, effort, and resilience—these are your best tools, not the instant illusions you once relied on."

A soft warmth spread through the clearing, and the sky above them cleared to reveal countless stars overhead—like a silent applause from Veritas itself. Sami, Mira, and Jax shared relieved, satisfied smiles, ready to continue onward.

<u>Mira's Field Note 3</u>
Title: "Completion Feels...Good?"
Notes:

- Spent hours shaping a phoenix statue. My arms ache, but it turned out more detailed than anything I've ever conjured instantly in digital spaces.

- Jax's bridge is incredibly sturdy—he overcame a ton of doubt.

- Sami's tower glowed at the end (the environment responding to us?). Evidence that Veritas rewards real perseverance?

Personal Thought:
We're exhausted, but there's this unexpected spark of pride. It's like discovering a secret about ourselves we didn't know.

The question now: how many more challenges does Veritas hold?

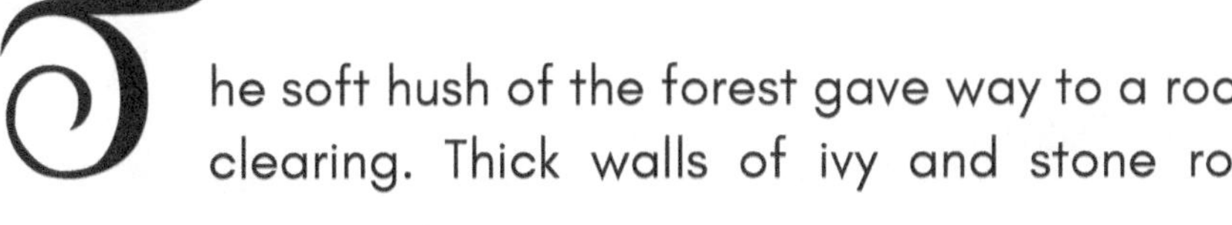

CHAPTER 4

The Labyrinth of Choices

he soft hush of the forest gave way to a rocky clearing. Thick walls of ivy and stone rose ahead in a winding pattern that seemed to stretch endlessly.

Jax let out a low whistle. "That's... a lot of stone. Could they not just have built a *tiny* maze?"

Elara, standing near a carved pillar, gave him a patient smile. "This is the Labyrinth of Choices. The size isn't to intimidate you—though it can. It's to remind you that each path shapes your journey in unexpected ways."

She stepped aside, revealing an archway of twisted roots leading into the maze. A faint glow illuminated ancient inscriptions along the walls, depicting stories of past travelers who braved their own labyrinth trials.

Mira brushed her fingertips over the symbols. "Look at these carvings... They show people picking between two paths, again and again. See? That one's shaped like an hourglass, and that one looks like a lightning bolt."

Elara nodded. "Indeed. Each choice can reveal an aspect of who you are—or who you might become. Heed the lessons learned in the Creations of Patience. Remember: not every short, wide road leads to success, nor does every narrow path end in failure."

She placed a hand on Sami's shoulder. "Trust yourselves. Trust each other." With that, she vanished, leaving only the quiet rustle of wind against ivy-laden walls.

The Maze Begins

Sami swallowed, peering at the entrance. "All right. We survived building statues, towers, and bridges. We can handle a few winding corridors."

Jax, arms folded, gave a half-laugh. "Sure… as long as we don't starve in here and start nibbling on moss for dinner."

Mira raised an eyebrow. "Your faith in our navigational skills is *staggering*."

Together, they walked through the labyrinth's threshold. Immediately, the world shifted: the forest noise faded, replaced by an eerie silence that made the scraping of their footsteps echo loudly.

Two Paths Diverge

They came to the first fork: a wide, brightly lit passage and a narrow, dimly lit corridor.

Jax glanced from one to the other, adjusting his glasses (which had begun to fog in the humid air). "So… big and bright or narrow and spooky?"

Mira shone a small flashlight from her pack down the narrower path. "I'm leaning spooky."

Jax faked a dramatic shudder. "Of course you are."

Sami exhaled, recalling Elara's guidance. "Yeah. Let's try the path that *isn't* obviously easy. We're not in Veritas to skip challenges, right?"

Mira: "Exactly. If it was easy, they wouldn't call it a *labyrinth*—they'd call it a *pleasant stroll*."

With mild grumbling from Jax, they ventured into the narrower passage. The walls forced them to walk single file, vines catching at their clothes. The air felt thick and musty, smelling faintly of earth and old stone.

A Surprising Detour

Around the next corner, they stumbled into an open courtyard lit by a shaft of sunlight through a break in the labyrinth ceiling. A small fountain babbled in the center, clear water trickling over mossy rocks. The corridor continued on the other side.

Jax eyed the fountain. "Water break?" he asked hopefully.

Mira knelt, testing the water's clarity. "It seems clean." She splashed a bit on her face, letting out a relieved sigh. "Refreshing—and not digital. Crazy, right?"

Sami joined them, cupping water in his hands to drink. The cool sensation against his lips reminded him how *real* Veritas was compared to the airy illusions of SandCraft. "Tastes... like an actual mountain spring."

As they stood, re-energized, they noticed an inscription near the fountain:

When dryness chokes you, choose to pause and drink.
When stillness tempts you, remember to keep moving.

Mira read it aloud. "Guess it's telling us not to linger too long in comfort."

Jax slung his backpack over his shoulder, smirking. "Yeah, yeah, no fun allowed. Message received." He winked. "Still, at least we're hydrated."

With a burst of shared laughter, they resumed their trek through the winding corridors.

The Doors: Gold vs. Wood

After several twists and turns (and at least two comedic dead ends—one featuring a talking raven statue that only cawed "Wrong way, genius!" whenever

Jax tried to pass), they finally reached a small clearing. There, two ornate doors stood side by side:

1. A door of pure gold, shimmering and lavish, carved with images of crowns and jewels.
2. A humble wooden door, weathered, with only a simple handle.

Jax let out a low whistle. "That gold door practically screams 'pick me, I'm important.'"

Sami studied the wooden door carefully. "We know from the last challenge that the obvious choice isn't always best."

Mira rapped her knuckles on the wooden surface. "Feels solid. The gold door might look fancy, but I'm guessing it's either locked or leads to some trap. This entire labyrinth is about making thoughtful choices, right?"

The three stood in a brief silence, considering. Then:

Sami: "Look, we were taught to stay humble. The gold door? That's too flashy."

Jax rubbed his neck. "All right, *fine*. But if the wooden door leads to a pit of vipers, I reserve the right to say 'I told you so'... even while being bitten."

Mira shoved the door open, rolling her eyes with a grin. "Deal. Let's go."

With a rusty creak, the wooden door opened onto a hidden chamber, radiant with warm light. Rows of ancient books lined stone shelves, and intricate scrolls were laid out on tables. A gentle breeze—smelling of parchment and sunlit dust—rustled the pages.

At the center stood a pedestal supporting a single, elaborately decorated scroll. Mira's eyes sparkled. "Jackpot," she whispered, carefully picking it up.

She unrolled the scroll, revealing flowing script:

> *"The greatest rewards are often hidden behind humble choices."*

> Sami felt a wave of validation wash over him. "Looks like we chose wisely."

A familiar voice broke the silence. Elara stood by one of the shelves, smiling. "You have shown both restraint and insight. Embrace humility, even when temptation glitters all around you. It will serve you well in Veritas—and beyond."

> Jax, swiping imaginary sweat from his forehead: "I'll be honest, I was preparing my speech for the *'pit of vipers' scenario.*"

Elara chuckled softly. "There are many kinds of pitfalls here, dear Jax—but you've proven you can navigate wisely."

<u>Mira's Field Note 4</u>

Title: "Maze or MADDENING Maze?"

Observations:

- Multiple routes tested our patience, big-time.

- The fountain's inscription: "Don't rest too long in comfort." Seems relevant to real life.

- The two doors highlight a theme of humility vs. temptation.

Funny Moments:

- Raven statue calling Jax a "genius" (sarcasm).

- Jax complaining he'd be snacking on moss.

- Sami's face when we found the fountain—pure relief!

Conclusion: The labyrinth is more than a puzzle—it's a reflection of our instincts. Must remember to stay open-minded... and keep an ear out for sassy ravens.

CHAPTER 5

Reflections and Revelations

A gentle wind stirred the meadow's wildflowers, sending a soft rustling sound across the field. The golden sunlight gave the clearing an ethereal quality, as though Veritas itself was holding its breath for what would happen next.

Sami, Mira, and Jax followed Elara across the meadow, each thoughtful after their triumph in the labyrinth. The group halted at an ancient stone well, its surface intricately carved with shifting symbols that caught the light.

Elara turned to them, voice calm yet tinged with solemnity. "This is the Well of Reflections. It shows not just your face, but the truth your heart most needs to see."

Jax raised an eyebrow, clearly uneasy. "Sounds... personal."

Elara nodded gently. "Often, the hardest journey is the one that leads inside ourselves."

The Glimpse Into Skyhaven

Sami approached the well first. Its surface appeared still, reflecting the sky overhead. But as he leaned closer, the image rippled and changed, revealing a ghostly version of Skyhaven—his old, perfect sandbox world. He saw it pristine, yet... strangely lifeless.

"Why does it look *so* empty?" Sami's brow furrowed. "I spent ages designing every detail."

Elara stood beside him. "Because perfection without challenge can feel hollow. You've realized the excitement fades when there's nothing to truly strive for."

Sami swallowed, the memory of summoning entire structures in seconds flashing through his mind. "I thought it would make me proud, but now it just... looks boring."

He stepped back, letting the image fade. A new determination flared within him—he wanted his creations to mean something, not just exist in a few effortless snaps.

Mira's Memories of Discovery

Mira took her turn next. She leaned over the well's rim, bracing herself for whatever she might see. In the still water, a younger version of herself shimmered into view, tinkering with a homemade robot in her parents' garage. She watched this younger Mira beam brightly at every small success—and even at some of the messier failures.

> Mira smiled, nostalgia lighting her eyes. "I remember that day. I got so frustrated because the robot's arm kept falling off." She chuckled. "But I never felt more alive than when I finally figured out how to fix it."

> Elara offered a gentle smile. "Real-world challenges, real-world solutions. You thrived on experimentation, and each misstep taught you something new."

Mira stood up, her heart warm with the memory. "Yeah... I guess I needed to be reminded of why I *like* real building so much."

Jax and the Fear of Giving Up

Jax hesitated at the well's edge, swallowing hard. "I— uh, guess it's my turn." His reflection in the water wavered, showing him as he was... then transforming into an older, tired version. This older Jax seemed weighed down, eyes dull. It looked like someone who had given up at every hurdle, content to live in the shadows of easy solutions.

Jax felt a chill race through him. "Is that... me? If I just keep running from challenges?"

Elara spoke softly, "Only if you *choose* to be. The future is not set in stone. Each decision shapes who you become."

Mira gently placed a hand on Jax's arm. "We won't let you give up," she murmured. "We've got your back, remember?"

Jax managed a shaky smile. "I appreciate it. Guess... I needed to see this to know what I *don't* want to become."

Renewed Purpose

With a quiet hush, the reflections faded away, and the water returned to its calm, mirror-like state. Sami, Mira, and Jax stepped back from the well, each looking both shaken and somehow *lighter*.

Sami let out a breath he didn't realize he'd been holding. "I feel... weirdly relieved. Like now I *really* know I don't want an empty paradise or a quick fix."

Jax rubbed his forehead. "And I don't want to coast on half-effort. Seeing that disappointed version of me... I'm going to work twice as hard to avoid that path."

Mira tucked a stray strand of hair behind her ear. "For me, it's remembering the rush of building something *real*. The Well sort of reminded me that my best inventions happened *after* I messed up a bunch of times."

Elara watched them all, pride clear in her gentle features. "You have faced your truths, and you stand stronger for it. Now, your final challenge awaits—one that will ask you to use everything you've learned about patience, cooperation, and authenticity."

Sami nodded. "We're ready."

Jax flashed a crooked grin. "I might be nervous, but hey, I'm in."

Mira crossed her arms confidently. "Let's do this—whatever 'final challenge' means in Veritas."

Elara led them away from the Well of Reflections, deeper into the meadow. As they traveled, a new energy crackled through the air—anticipation mingled with a sense of imminent discovery. In the fading daylight, the wildflowers seemed to turn their faces toward the trio, as if saluting their courage.

<u>Mira's Field Note 5</u>

Title: "Looking in the Mirror—and Not Liking What You See?"

Key Moments:

- Sami's memory of Skyhaven—perfect but lifeless.

- My childhood self, so enthusiastic about real-world tinkering.

- Jax seeing his potential future if he stops trying. Gave him quite a scare!

My Thoughts:

- Veritas keeps showing us that illusions are hollow compared to real effort.
- I'm proud of Jax—he's stepping up despite his doubts. Sami too: you can tell he's got this new fire inside him.
- Elara mentioned a "final challenge"—what does that even look like? And are we truly ready for it?

CHAPTER 6

Heart of Veritas

A fresh, cool breeze brushed against Sami's cheeks as he, Mira, and Jax followed Elara up the winding path. The gentle meadow below had gradually transformed into rugged terrain—a slope dotted with jagged rocks and wisps of mist. Each step higher seemed to intensify the electric energy in the air, as though the mountaintop was pulling them forward.

Jax, panting slightly, paused to rest his hands on his knees. "Are we sure we can't just build, I don't know, a convenient escalator? My legs are going on strike."

Mira shot him an amused glance. "Sure, let's conjure a *magic elevator* while we're at it. Because we haven't learned *anything* about the value of effort..."

Sami grinned, offering Jax a hand. "Come on, big guy. This is the last stretch—don't want to miss the grand finale."

As they pressed on, the path leveled out into a wide plateau. Towering stone pillars circled a grand platform etched with runes, each symbol faintly glowing. At the center, an enormous crystal pulsed with an otherworldly light, vibrant and alive—the Heart of Veritas.

The Final Challenge Revealed

Elara guided them to the edge of the platform. Her expression was calm but carried a hint of gravity. "You stand before the Heart of Veritas. It holds the balance between imagination, effort, patience, and reality." She met each of their gazes in turn. "Your final challenge is to restore that balance—within the crystal and within yourselves."

Jax exhaled nervously, glancing at the pillars. "So... is there a puzzle? A hidden lever? Some big boss monster?"

Elara shook her head gently. "No puzzle or monster—at least, not in a literal sense. You must combine everything you have learned to connect with the Heart of Veritas. It will respond only to true unity and understanding."

The trio exchanged determined looks. Sami took the lead, stepping onto the platform until he stood before the crystal. It shone with prismatic brilliance, reflecting every color of the spectrum in constant, graceful motion. Mira and Jax joined him, each placing a hand on the crystal's smooth surface.

A Surge of Memory and Magic

The moment their fingers touched the crystal, energy flared around them, warm yet electric. Instantly, vivid images flashed through their minds:

- The Creations of Patience: Stone phoenix wings, a rebuilt bridge, a spiral tower—reminders of real effort.
- The Labyrinth of Choices: Narrow paths, tricky doors, the lesson of humility.
- The Well of Reflections: Confronting illusions, discovering personal truths.

Sami felt his heart pound in rhythm with the crystal. Each memory merged into a single, powerful realization: the best creations—like the best choices—come with struggle, patience, and honesty.

Mira's voice sounded distant, echoing inside his mind. "It's like all our experiences are weaving together..."

Jax let out a shaky laugh. "I've never felt so... aware. Everything we've done is reminding me how far we've come."

The crystal responded to their unity, glowing brighter with each beat of their shared understanding. Suddenly, a wave of light burst from its core, expanding over the platform and surging across Veritas in a magnificent ripple. The pillars' runes flared brilliantly, their patterns dancing across the night sky in arcs of colorful luminescence.

A Flicker of Shadow

Yet as the energy faded, Sami noticed a tiny flicker of darkness at the crystal's center—barely visible, but distinctly present. A chill coursed down his spine. Though the crystal shone with renewed balance, this small spot of shadow hinted at something unresolved.

Sami glanced at Elara, alarmed. "The crystal... did you see that?"

For a fleeting moment, Elara's serene face flickered with worry. Then she smiled, though it didn't reach her eyes. "You have done wonderfully—better than any in a long time. The Heart of Veritas is stronger now, thanks to you."

Jax, eyeing the crystal warily: "But what was that flicker?"

Elara gently shook her head. "Balance is never a permanent state. Shadows can remain, waiting for the right moment. Remember this feeling of unity you share now—it will guide you if darkness ever returns."

Sami felt conflicting emotions swirl inside: triumph at having completed the challenge, and a nagging unease about the lingering shadow.

The Descent

At last, Elara motioned for them to descend. With one final, awestruck glance at the Heart of Veritas, Sami followed Jax and Mira down a winding stair carved into the rock. The air grew warmer the farther they got from the summit, yet his mind remained on that strange flicker of darkness.

Mira nudged him, her tone reassuring. "Hey, don't overthink it. We did a *lot* of good up there."

Sami exhaled slowly. "Yeah... I just can't shake the feeling something else is coming."

Jax, trying to lighten the mood, smirked. "Well, bring it on. We've faced illusions, labyrinths, and precarious stone towers. We're practically pros now."

Their voices carried across the mountainside, echoing faintly, as Veritas itself seemed to listen. And in the sky above, the pillars atop the summit glowed softly, as if standing guard.

<u>Mira's Field Note 6</u>

Title: "The Day We Touched the Heart"

Observations:

- The crystal pulses like a living heart—responded to our combined memories.

- Saw a shadow inside. Could be leftover negativity or unbalanced energy? Must investigate more if we can.

- Jax asked about a "boss monster," which is hilarious and also terrifying—no thanks!

Personal Takeaway:

- Teamwork = Real magic.
- Balance can be restored, but maybe it's never guaranteed forever... is that the next lesson?

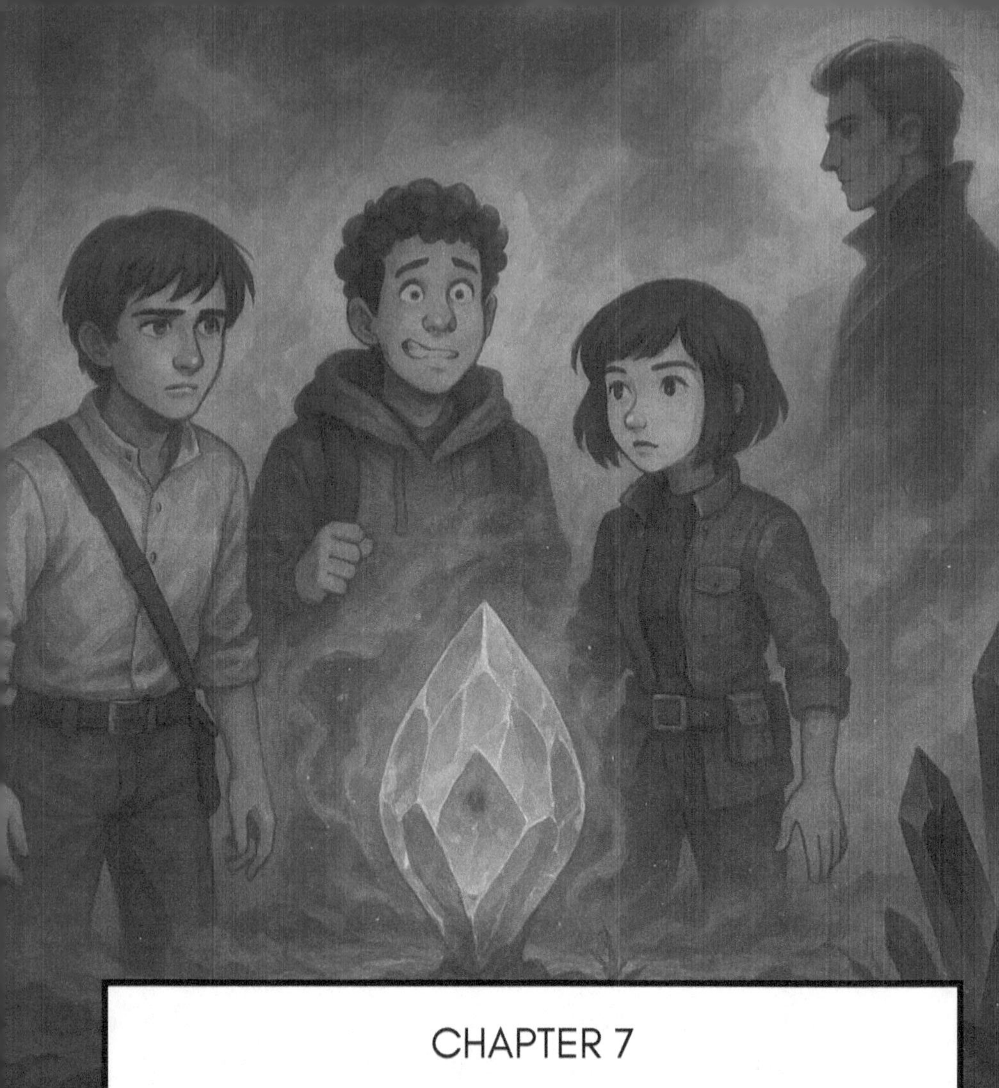

CHAPTER 7

Shadows of Doubt

A soft rumble of thunder rolled across the distant skies as Sami, Mira, and Jax descended from the mountaintop, hearts still pounding with the lingering thrill of the Heart of Veritas. Yet with each step downward, the mood shifted. The once vibrant, sunlit meadow at the base now lay shrouded in an unnatural, clammy fog.

Sami hugged his arms, feeling an icy prickle at the back of his neck. "It was sunny just an hour ago. How did this fog roll in so fast?"

Mira squinted, her normally keen eyes struggling to pierce the haze. "Something's off. Almost...like the land is reacting to that shadow in the crystal."

Jax forced a laugh, though his voice wavered. "You're both being overly dramatic—maybe it's just weird mountain weather...right?"

Sami and Mira exchanged a look. They knew this was no simple weather shift.

Nagging Uncertainty

As they continued, Sami couldn't shake the image of that flicker in the crystal's depths. Was it an omen? A remnant of something bigger?

Sami finally broke the silence. "That black speck we saw—did it feel... alive to you?"

Mira gave a solemn nod. "Yeah. Like a stain on something pure. It definitely didn't belong."

Jax, picking at a loose thread on his sleeve: "So, we purified the Heart of Veritas *mostly*, but maybe not entirely?"

A faint, echoing voice drifted on the wind—Elara's warning:

"Something in Veritas has been disturbed. Remain vigilant."

Encounter with Caius

Through the swirling mist, a lithe figure emerged—sharp features, piercing gaze, and a charismatic half-smile that didn't quite reach his eyes. He wore a sleek cloak embroidered with faintly glowing patterns, reminiscent of Elara's style but twisted in design.

Sami instinctively stepped between him and his friends. "Who are you?"

"Caius," the stranger said smoothly, tipping his head in mock greeting. "I see you've been meddling in the affairs of Veritas. Restoring balance, are we?"

Mira scoffed, crossing her arms. "Somebody had to fix what you broke, apparently."

Caius let out a soft, humorless chuckle. "Veritas isn't broken—it's just *limited*. Why waste energy on patience and effort when you could have everything instantly, any world you desire, *no strings attached*?"

Jax shuffled uncomfortably, remembering how tempting that idea used to be. But he forced himself to speak up. "We've tried instant. It's empty."

Caius's gaze flicked to Jax, as though sizing him up. "Empty—until you realize what true *power* feels like."

Sami felt a chill crawl over his skin. "Power at what cost?" he challenged. "We've learned something you'll never understand: the struggle *matters*."

With a lazy wave of his hand, Caius dissolved into the mist, leaving only his final words echoing:

"Come find me when you're ready for *real* potential."

Into the Fog

An uneasy silence followed Caius's departure. The fog thickened, muffling their footsteps. A sudden glimmer in the grass caught Jax's eye—a crystal shard, glowing softly with enchanting blues and purples. Something about it called to him, whispering promises of ease.

Jax reached out, mind drifting dreamily. "Maybe...just a little look—"

"Jax, wait!" Mira lunged, grabbing his wrist before he could touch it. "That thing's practically screaming *'trap!'*"

Sami knelt beside the shard, heart pounding from the near-miss. "It looks like one of Caius's illusions, designed to lure you in."

Jax stood back, face pale. "I—I barely realized I was reaching for it." He shuddered. "That's scary."

Mira gently pried the shard free, wrapping it in a cloth. "We'll analyze it later. Let's keep moving before more nasty surprises show up."

Signs of Disturbance

They pressed on through the swirling mist, noticing more strange occurrences:

- A flower patch turning black around the edges, petals curling unnaturally.
- Shafts of cracked earth, as if something stirred beneath the surface.
- A warped statue they passed earlier now partially crumbled.

Mira, eyeing the withered foliage: "It's like Veritas itself is sick."

Sami nodded, jaw clenched. "Caius is behind this. He must be tapping the realm's energy to spread illusions."

Jax, swallowing thickly: "We need Elara. Maybe she can help us figure out a plan."

Yet, Elara's voice only flickered in and out, echoing faintly with words of caution. The trio realized they might be on their own—for now.

<u>Mira's Field Note 7</u>
Title: "Fog and Fears"
Observations:

- Encountered a mysterious guy named Caius—apparently an ex-Architect or something?

- Found a suspicious, glowing shard nearly lured Jax in. We suspect illusions are spreading.

- The environment: blackened flowers, cracked ground. Definitely not normal Veritas vibes.

Personal Concern:

- If Caius is causing these disturbances, how far can he go?
- Elara's voice is fading. Are we losing contact with her?

CHAPTER 8

Whispers of Temptation

A gloomy twilight gripped Veritas, the sky swirling uneasily with shades of crimson and charcoal. Sami, Mira, and Jax moved forward cautiously, sensing an oppressive tension in the thick air, as though unseen eyes followed their every step.

Jax fidgeted nervously, gripping the torch tightly. "Are we sure we can't, like, build some protective bubble around us?"

Mira sighed, placing a comforting hand on his shoulder. "We'd need to earn protection here. This isn't SandCraft, remember?"

Sami offered Jax a reassuring smile. "Besides, shortcuts haven't exactly worked out for us."

They exchanged weak chuckles, pushing on with determination tempered by recent experiences.

The Shimmering Cavern

The path suddenly widened into a vast cavern shimmering with crystals of every imaginable color. Torchlight danced across countless facets, throwing mesmerizing patterns onto the floor.

Mira gasped softly, eyes widening with awe. "It's like walking inside a giant prism."

Jax nodded slowly, admiration mingling with anxiety. "Amazing—but we know pretty things here usually mean trouble."

"Stay alert," Sami cautioned. "Don't touch anything until we're sure it's safe."

The cavern felt strangely alive, crystals subtly shifting hues, reflecting their emotions—curiosity, wonder, caution—pulsing softly around them.

Jax's Temptation

They reached an alcove shaped like an arched doorway. At its center, a blue crystal radiated an enchanting glow.

Jax's breathing quickened. "Have you ever seen something so...perfect?"

Sami felt immediate alarm. "Jax—careful!"

But Jax, eyes glazed, reached out as if entranced. As soon as his fingertips brushed the crystal, tendrils of blue energy wrapped tightly around his wrist, drawing him in.

Jax's mind plunged into a dreamlike world, where entire cities rose effortlessly from his imagination. No failures. No effort. Only ease and endless power.

"Stay..." a silky voice whispered. "Anything you wish... instantly yours."

"Jax, snap out of it!" Mira shouted, panic gripping her. She grabbed Jax's arm and pulled desperately.

Sami lunged forward, shielding his eyes. "Pull him back, Mira!" he yelled. Together, they tore Jax away from the crystal.

The blue energy shattered, dissolving into harmless sparks. Jax stumbled backward, gasping and shaking, confusion clouding his eyes.

"What... what happened?" he stammered, sweat beading his forehead. "It felt so real... so easy. I'm sorry, guys."

Mira steadied him, relief clear in her voice. "You're safe now—that's what matters."

Sami's heart pounded. "Another trap. Caius is trying harder than ever to exploit our weaknesses."

Illusion vs. Reality

The friends paused to regroup, eyes wary. Now the crystals, though beautiful, clearly marked danger.

Mira frowned deeply. "This cave reflects desires. It gives you what you want—without any work."

Sami nodded grimly. "Exactly what we've learned to resist."

Jax, voice strained but firm: "From now on, we stick together. No more falling for illusions."

Renewed determination filled them. They advanced cautiously, carefully avoiding temptation, each wary sparkle a possible threat. Their teamwork strengthened, each vigilant for signs of another trap.

Caius Watches

Unseen, hidden in shadows deeper in the cavern, Caius observed their careful steps. A faint, menacing smile curved his lips.

"Such stubbornness," he murmured softly. "But soon, you'll see: instant power always defeats patience."

His mocking laughter echoed faintly as he vanished, unnoticed by the trio below.

Emerging Stronger

Finally stepping out into the cool night air, the friends breathed deep sighs of relief. Stars glinted softly in the indigo sky, though the day's trials weighed heavily on their hearts.

Jax slumped against a rock, running a shaky hand through his hair. "Too close. If you guys weren't here..."

Mira knelt beside him, eyes gentle yet resolute. "We're a team, Jax. Always."

Sami stared thoughtfully back at the cavern. "We need Elara's help. Caius is getting more dangerous. We have to be ready."

Cautious but strengthened by their experience, the three moved forward, knowing that together, they could resist any illusion Caius tried to throw their way.

<u>Mira's Field Note 8</u>

Title: "Crystal Cave of Doom... Or Something"

Key Observations:

- Hypnotic crystals that lock you in illusions of effortless power—beyond dangerous.

- Jax nearly got trapped in a perfect fantasy. He's shaken but okay now.

- Caius is lurking—definitely messing with us.

Personal Thoughts:

- I realize any of us could fall for these illusions if we drop our guard.
- Trusting each other is the best defense.

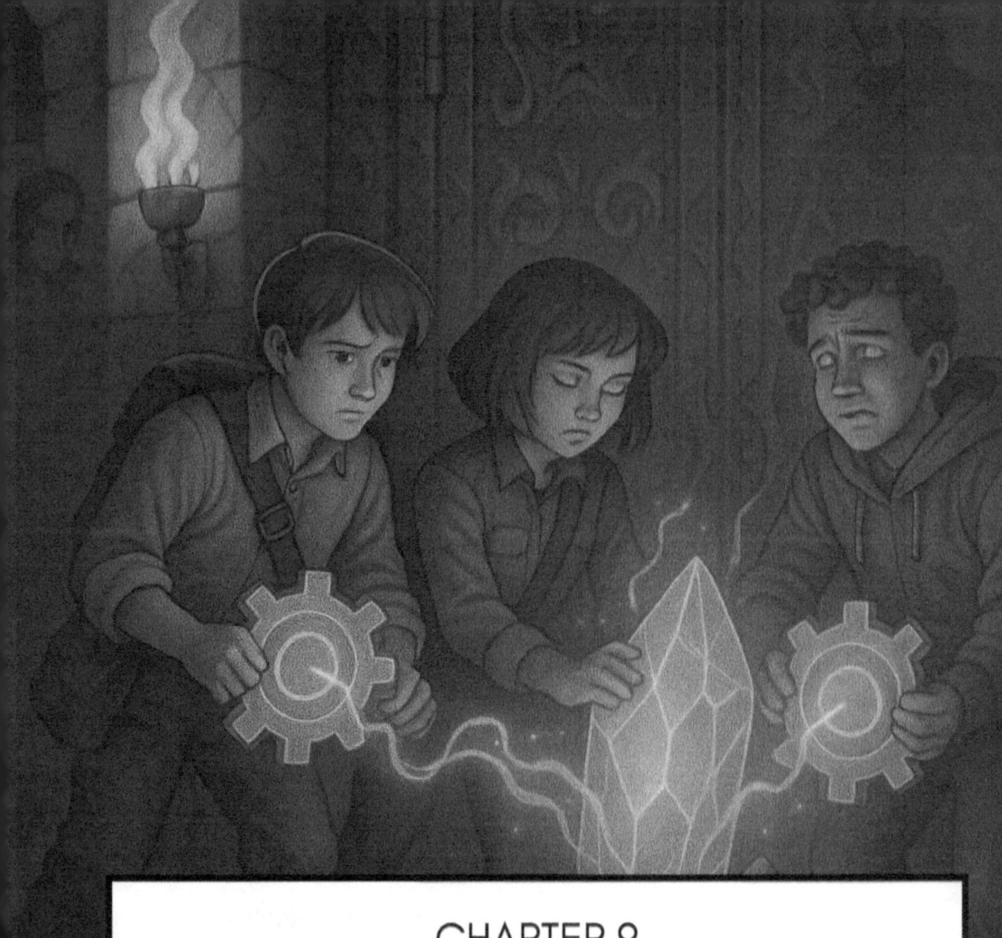

CHAPTER 9

Secrets of the Shadows

Beneath the blood-tinged sunset, Sami, Mira, and Jax traversed a rocky pathway that led to a looming black-stone temple—its towering spires cutting stark silhouettes against the twilight sky. The ancient symbols etched into the temple walls seemed to pulse with faint silver light, as though awakened by their approach.

Jax, taking in the ominous surroundings, murmured, "Raise your hand if you wish we'd stayed in that cozy meadow…"

Mira smirked, shoving him lightly. "And miss out on discovering *whatever monstrosity* lurks here? No thanks."

Sami forced a chuckle, his heart hammering despite the banter. "We've tackled illusions and labyrinths, right? This is just another step."

Nonetheless, their playful words did little to dispel the growing sense of foreboding. Flickers of half-remembered warnings from Elara and the sinister presence of Caius haunted their thoughts.

The Temple's Gloomy Halls

Inside, the temple walls rose high, carved with swirling murals depicting heroes of old conquering monstrous threats—or forging creations with blood, sweat, and tears. Torches sputtered in brackets, casting dancing shadows that made the carvings appear to come alive.

Mira peered at one panel showing a cloaked figure chiseling a giant statue by hand. "Look, they took ages just to finish that piece. We've definitely learned that feeling."

Jax, still uneasy, drifted close to Sami. "Yeah, but those guys *won*, right?" He paused, eyeing another carving of a monstrous shape looming behind the hero. "At least I hope so…"

Sami nodded, scanning the engraved battle scenes. "All these images… They highlight real commitment over shortcuts."

A cold draft swept past, stirring the torch flames and making them flicker restlessly.

The Obsidian Door & Puzzle

At last, they reached a massive obsidian door, its surface so polished it almost mirrored their faces. Interlocking gears, strange runes, and a carved riddle covered the stone:

> To proceed, solve this trial three—
> Each alone fails; united you'll be free.
> Turn your gears in perfect sync—
> Patience binds stronger than you think.

Jax, reading the inscription: "I guess it's one of those 'team synergy or bust' deals, huh?"

Mira traced a faintly glowing rune with her fingertip. "We've done this sort of thing before. But something tells me there's a twist."

Sami squared his shoulders. "Well, let's find out."

Each friend placed a hand on a separate gear, the stone cold beneath their palms. Instantly, the runes flared, and a deep, resonant voice filled the corridor:

"Match your pace with mind and heart,
Turn the gears to do your part.
Hurry alone, the puzzle resets—
United, you shall pass its test."

Trial of Unity

They began turning the gears. At first, the mechanism groaned in protest if they moved too quickly or jerkily. The slightest misalignment sent the whole contraption resetting, causing a chorus of clanking metal and glowing runes to blink in disapproval.

Jax let out a frustrated groan. "We're not robots— how do we keep perfect time?"

Mira inhaled slowly, letting the tension settle. "Remember the spiral tower? The labyrinth? We found our rhythm together."

Sami closed his eyes, nodding. "Let's slow our breathing. Match each other. Don't overthink."

They tried again, each rotating the gear with deliberate, steady movements. When one gear squeaked or met resistance, the others paused, adjusting until they found the sweet spot. It took patience—each slip threatened to send them back to square one.

Minutes ticked by, or perhaps hours. The swirling runes flickered between bright azure and frustrated crimson, as though sensing their progress and setbacks. Time seemed suspended in that cold corridor, the only sounds being the click of gears, stifled groans, and the rasp of their breathing.

Finally:

Clink-click... clink-click... The gears locked into place, smoothly aligned.

A soft hum filled the air, and the door shuddered. With a deep, resonant thrum, it slid open, revealing a spiraling staircase stretching downward. Torches along the walls sprang to life in a cascade of flickering flames.

Jax slumped in relief, wiping sweat off his brow. "We did it? Yes! I was about three seconds away from elbow-dropping this puzzle."

Sami clapped him on the back. "Team synergy for the win."

Mira, grinning, stepped forward. "Let's see what's below—before anything decides to reset on us."

Descent into Darkness

Gripping the railing for balance, they descended. The air grew colder, smelling faintly of damp stone and something vaguely metallic, like iron. Their torches sputtered as if complaining about the depths. Tension pressed in around them.

Sami spared a glance back up the staircase. "Feels like we're going into the heart of the temple. Or maybe the *belly of the beast.*"

Jax, forcing a laugh: "As long as no actual beasts show up, I'm good."

But as they moved deeper, whispers seemed to drift from the walls, echoing in a hush of voices. Caius's presence stirred at the edges of their awareness—though they couldn't see him, his mocking energy felt closer than ever.

<u>Mira's Field Note 9</u>

Title: "Obsidian Trials & Team Gears"

Observations:

- The door puzzle demanded perfect coordination—no place for rushing.

- The glowing runes seemed to "react" to our synergy (or lack thereof).

- Carvings in the temple show legendary figures accomplishing feats through real grit... possibly a warning (or encouragement?)

Personal Take:

- We're growing more comfortable with each other's rhythms—especially Jax. who ironically wants to rush but can adapt when needed.
- There's a dark presence here. Caius? Or something older?

CHAPTER 10

Echoes of the Past

Leaving the towering black-stone temple behind, Sami, Mira, and Jax emerged into the cool twilight of Veritas. Their breaths formed faint clouds in the crisp air, and each step felt heavier, as though the depths they'd ventured into clung to them like a stubborn shadow.

Elara guided them through winding paths that glowed softly under the moonlight. The forest canopy overhead swayed, whispering ancient secrets. Bit by bit, the tension from the temple gave way to a different kind of anticipation—a calm before a greater storm.

Sami, glancing at Elara's serene expression: "Where are we going now? More illusions? Another puzzle?"

Elara shook her head gently. "No illusions, no gears. This trial comes not from outside, but from within."

Jax, still wrestling with a knot of nerves, forced a grin. "Great... *internal struggles* are my favorite."

Mira shot him a half-smile, though her eyes sparkled with sympathy.

The Twilight Grove

At last, they emerged into a tranquil grove bathed in the gentle light of dusk. White wildflowers blanketed the ground, their petals glinting like tiny stars. In the center stood an enormous, ancient tree, its trunk so wide that ten people holding hands wouldn't span its circumference. The bark was etched with countless symbols—spirals, runes, and intricate shapes, each telling a silent story.

Elara, voice hushed with reverence: "This is the Tree of Echoes. Here, you must confront the past you carry, the doubts that linger, and the fears that shape your choices."

Sami, Mira, and Jax exchanged uneasy glances. Despite the peaceful setting, the gravity of Elara's words made their hearts pound. Yet all three understood they hadn't come this far to turn back.

Confronting Sami's Past

Sami approached first. Steeling himself, he pressed his palm against the rough bark. Instantly, the grooves and symbols seemed to pulse, and a rush of memories flooded his mind:

1. Skyhaven, conjured in seconds—perfect yet hollow.
2. His frustration whenever something took longer than expected.
3. The pang of jealousy or boredom when others in the real world actually *built* with patience.

Within these visions, he saw how fleeting those instant successes felt. They left him wanting more, never truly satisfied.

Sami whispered, tears prickling at his eyes, "I relied on shortcuts... believed that speed and perfection were all that mattered."

He inhaled shakily. "But real strength... it grows when we work, when we fail, when we try again."

A comforting warmth blossomed in his chest—like the tree *approved* of his revelation. Slowly, he stepped back, face set with new resolve.

Mira's Memories of Standing Out

With a slight tremor in her hand, Mira touched the tree next. For a heartbeat, nothing happened. Then a wave of emotions washed over her:

1. Childhood: building tiny robots, rummaging through recycling bins for spare parts—peers mocking her "weird" hobby.
2. The isolation she sometimes felt for preferring real-world tinkering over popular sandbox games.
3. Glimpses of the *fulfillment* she experienced every time a homemade gadget finally whirred to life.

She remembered reading about Veritas in old e-zines, dreaming of a place that celebrated creativity shaped by real effort. A faint ache tugged at her heart—memories of being misunderstood, teased, or simply ignored.

Mira exhaled, tears forming at the corners of her eyes. "I thought being different made me lonely. But that difference is my strength... I see that now."

Her lips curved into a smile. "No more doubting that I belong."

The tree's engravings glowed softly under her touch, as if acknowledging her discovery.

Jax's Struggle with Self-Doubt

Finally, Jax approached, hands trembling more than he'd care to admit. He pressed a sweaty palm to the ancient bark, bracing himself. In a rush of images, he saw:

1. The countless times he shrank away from challenges, letting Sami or Mira take the lead.
2. The embarrassment of messing up at tasks he never really tried to learn.
3. His longing to be truly *good* at something, not just riding on friends' successes.

He watched an older version of himself drift away from opportunities out of fear—a life of half-effort and regrets.

Jax felt a surge of emotion tighten his throat. "I don't want that. I don't want to... stay small just because I'm scared."

He swallowed. "Failure isn't the end if I keep going."

A gentle warmth radiated from the tree into his chest, stirring a sense of determination he'd never felt so strongly.

Emerging Stronger

One by one, they pulled back from the Tree of Echoes, feeling *lighter*—as if they'd dropped a heavy weight they hadn't realized they were carrying.

Elara, standing by with soft pride in her eyes: "You have each confronted your own truths. This acceptance arms you against illusions and gives Veritas the genuine energy it needs to heal."

Sami, Mira, and Jax met each other's gazes, relief and confidence shining through.

Mira murmured, "We still have to deal with Caius. But at least we know ourselves better now."

Jax nodded, squaring his shoulders. "We won't let fear or shortcuts define us."

Sami, setting a hand on both their shoulders: "Ready to face him—together?"

They all turned to Elara, who smiled warmly, her voice laced with respect. "You have taken yet another step toward restoring Veritas. Now, prepare yourselves for what's ahead. Caius will not yield easily."

With that, they left the tranquil grove behind, hearts steady despite the swirling unknowns ahead. If illusions and shortcuts had once tempted them, the Tree of Echoes reminded them of who they truly were—and what they could accomplish with unity and perseverance.

<u>Mira's Field Note 10</u>
Title: "Facing Our Inner Shadows"
Observations:

- The Tree of Echoes reacts to deep truths—like a mirror for the soul.

- We each have regrets or fears, but acknowledging them seems to free something inside us.

- Elara says these revelations fuel Veritas with genuine creative energy (no illusions needed!).

Personal Thoughts:

- Seeing how Jax doubted himself made me realize we all have hidden insecurities.

- Sami's admission about easy wins vs. real pride was powerful.

- We're more united than ever—Caius, watch out.

CHAPTER 11

Into the Real

Clara led Sami, Mira, and Jax away from the Tree of Echoes, their newly affirmed courage burning bright. Yet each step into the deeper recesses of Veritas brought an unsettling shift—colors once vivid dulled to muted tones, paths once clear fractured into ever-changing trails, and the warm breezes turned sharp and chilly.

Jax, hugging his jacket closer: "Is it just me, or is Veritas...glitching?"

Elara glanced back, eyes somber. "Not exactly glitching. Caius is forcing reality and illusions to overlap, dismantling the realm's natural balance. If he succeeds, nothing in Veritas—nor your world— will feel truly real again."

Sami swallowed hard. It was as if the ground beneath them slanted unpredictably, the horizon warping whenever he looked too long.

Reality in Flux

Branches overhead bent at impossible angles; fallen leaves hovered midair momentarily before fluttering back to earth. One trail led to a swirling pool that vanished when they blinked. Each distortion reminded them of SandCraft illusions taken to a dangerous extreme.

Mira shuddered. "It's like we're stuck in a half-finished digital landscape. Everything feels... off."

Elara gestured to a twisting path. "Stay close. The illusions will try to split us up. We can't let that happen."

Jax, forcing a smirk: "Since when is 'split up' ever a good idea in a creepy setting?"

Sami felt a burst of gratitude for Jax's attempt at humor, even though dread curled in his stomach.

Caius Emerges

They ventured deeper, weaving past flickering illusions of towering spires and shadowy creatures that vanished as soon as they approached. Abruptly, the atmosphere crackled with energy, and Caius materialized, his cloak shimmering with the same unnatural glitching effect that plagued Veritas.

Caius, voice smooth: "Ah, my weary travelers. Ready to embrace a world without constraints?"

Elara's calm facade slipped just enough to reveal her tension. "Caius, this will destroy the essence of Veritas. You twist freedom into a weapon."

Caius arched an eyebrow, stepping forward. "Freedom *isn't* a weapon—it's a gift. No more waiting, no more slow-building nonsense. Create—and rule—instantly."

Sami felt a surge of anger. "We've seen where that leads: empty illusions that trap you, offering nothing real."

Caius shook his head, eyes glinting with scorn. "You say that now, but how long before you crave easy victories again?"

Warped Temptations

With a flick of Caius's wrist, shifting visions rose around them:

- Sami glimpsed a new, improved Skyhaven—vast and perfect. No frustration, no mistakes.
- Mira saw a flawless laboratory where every experiment succeeded instantly.
- Jax beheld a heroic version of himself, admired by everyone without the need for any actual perseverance.

The illusions shimmered, so *tantalizingly* close.

> Elara shouted over the swirling visions, voice resonating with power: "Remember who you are. These illusions target your fears and desires—don't let them consume you!"

Sami clenched his fists, ignoring the half-formed image of a golden city rising behind him. "I'm done with illusions."

> Mira, eyes narrowing, turned her back on the futuristic lab. "My best inventions were always messy first. I don't want guaranteed success."

Jax swallowed hard, stepping away from the image of his idolized self. "I'd rather be real—even if I fail—than hollow."

Caius's confident smirk quavered for just a heartbeat, but he quickly recovered. "You've grown, I'll grant you that. But you can't stop me from reshaping Veritas in my image."

With a swirl of crackling energy, he vanished into the distorting landscape once more, leaving them reeling.

The Breaking Point

The environment deteriorated further: trees bent in half, entire patches of land flickered between solid and transparent. Even Elara looked strained, her robes losing their soft glow.

> Elara exhaled shakily. "He's pushing the realm to its breaking point. We must find where he's anchoring this corruption and sever it."

> Sami, jaw set: "Point us in the right direction."

She led them through a labyrinth of half-formed illusions—false doorways, phantom creatures. The sky above roiled like storm clouds infected with neon static.

> Mira studied the shifting illusions, her inventor's mind racing. "Everything is flickering...like partial code. Maybe if we identify the main 'link' or anchor, we can disrupt it."

Jax gazed around, still shaken from earlier illusions. "If we fail—this entire place could collapse, right?"

Elara nodded solemnly. "Or remain locked in a permanent state of half-reality, half-illusion, pulling more minds into Caius's empty world."

That knowledge cast a chill over them, but it also fueled a fierce resolve. They had to confront Caius, no matter the cost.

<u>Mira's Field Note 11</u>
Title: "Blurring Lines"
Observations:

- Veritas is glitching—similar to a corrupted code or incomplete blueprint.

- Caius claims he offers "pure freedom," but we see illusions that strip away real effort.

- Elara seems more worried than ever—she's losing some of her calm glow.

Personal Thought:

- We almost caved at those illusions again. But remembering our growth from the Tree of Echoes saved us.
- Next step: finding Caius's anchor and stopping this chaos.

CHAPTER 12
Return to Reality

Wind howled across the fractured landscape of Veritas. The realm teetered between solid ground and swirling illusions, each glitching portion flickering like broken pixels. Sami, Mira, and Jax, accompanied by Elara, hurried onward under a sky streaked with unnatural hues of teal and magenta.

Mira, glancing up: "This place is warping more by the second. If we don't stop Caius soon—"

Elara, her voice tense, finished the thought. "Veritas may become a permanent illusion, bleeding into your reality as well."

Despite the urgency, the trio moved with renewed confidence, fueled by all they had endured and discovered about themselves. They knew one thing: illusions alone would never defeat them if they trusted each other and held tight to *real* creativity.

Confronting Caius

A jagged chasm opened up before them, beyond which lay a twisted fortress—Caius's makeshift stronghold. Tower-like columns reached into the swirling sky, each flickering between solid stone and shimmering code.

Jax, trying to lighten the mood: "Anyone else nostalgic for the Labyrinth of Choices instead of... *that?*"

Sami forced a grin. "I'll take real vines and puzzle doors over glitchy chaos any day."

Elara raised a hand. Light flared around her fingers, forming a bridge of woven energy across the chasm. "Caius's illusions can distort matter, but remain focused. This bridge is real enough to bear us if we believe in its purpose."

Step by careful step, they crossed the luminous pathway, the chasm below dropping into an endless swirl of illusions. At the fortress gates, Caius appeared, robes crackling with shimmering arcs of distorted power.

> Caius, cold amusement lacing his tone: "You're persistent. But you can't hold back a future of *limitless creation.*"

> Sami stood tall. "Limitless? More like meaningless."

> Mira added, "We'd rather build something real—flawed, maybe, but *ours.*"

Jax mustered a brave smirk. "Anyway, we've faced your illusions, so give it your best shot."

Caius sneered, raising his hand. "So be it."

Battle of Illusions vs. Reality

A sudden eruption of swirling illusions exploded from Caius's cloak:

1. Shifting platforms that rose and vanished beneath their feet, threatening to send them tumbling.

2. Phantom creatures lunging with blazing eyes, only to dissolve when struck with real determination.

3. Echoes of the trio's old temptations—flickers of a perfect Skyhaven, an effortless inventor's lab, a champion Jax. Each taunt tried to lure them off course.

Yet the group resisted:

- Mira unleashed her clever inventiveness: She hurled small mechanical orbs (crafted from leftover Veritas scraps) that stabilized the flickering ground.

- Jax braved the phantom beasts, batting away illusions by refusing to fear them. "You're not real!" he roared, letting them dissolve.

- Sami, recalling how he once loved instant creation, now wielded the *strength* of slow, methodical effort. Each time an illusion of easy victory beckoned, he turned his back on it, focusing on the *tangible* steps forward.

Elara guided them, channeling Veritas's pure energy to counter Caius's corruption. Her robes glowed again, color returning to the realm inch by inch.

The Heart of the Anchor

At the fortress's core stood a massive obsidian device, humming with the same half-real glitch effect. Runes twisted across its surface, tethering illusions to Veritas's living fabric.

> Caius poured all his will into it. "You want a perfect world... or do you fear greatness?"

> Sami, stepping toward the device, shook his head. "No... we've learned that perfection without effort is *hollow*."

> Mira added, "A world built on illusions falls apart the second you need something real."

> Jax, eyes steely, "And you can't scare us off with cheap temptations anymore."

With a surge of unified determination, the trio and Elara pressed their hands to the obsidian anchor, summoning the lessons they had gained: the Creations of Patience, the Labyrinth of Choices, the Well of Reflections, the trials of illusions. Real sweat, tears, triumphs—these overcame illusions in an instant.

> Elara's voice, resonating: "Veritas thrives on honest struggle, not conjured ease. Return to your source, illusions—begone!"

Power flared as a brilliant gold-white light erupted, coursing through the anchor. The runes hissed and shattered, illusions dissolving like mist in sunlight.

Caius's Downfall... and Escape

Caius staggered, cloak flickering. For a moment, a look of raw despair flickered in his eyes—then twisted to rage. "You'd trade unlimited possibility for *limitations*? Fools!"

> Sami met his gaze, resolute. "We'd rather earn our creations than live a lie."

The fortress walls began to crumble, glitching illusions collapsing under the anchor's destruction. Bits of code-like fragments cascaded around them. Caius gave one last, furious glare—then vanished into a spiral of swirling shadows, leaving only an echo of his voice:

> "You've won *this* round. But illusions are never truly gone..."

Restoring Veritas

As the fortress collapsed, the ground steadied. Trees in the distance regained their natural shape, the sky's chaotic swirl reverted to a golden dawn, and the fresh scent of untainted air filled their lungs. Veritas breathed anew, healing from the inside out.

Jax, letting out a whoop: "Ha! The illusions are gone!"

Mira exhaled, shoulders sagging with relief. "We did it. Feels... unbelievably *real*."

Elara approached, gratitude shining in her eyes. "By choosing genuine creativity—by facing challenges instead of chasing shortcuts—you've restored the soul of Veritas."

Sami, Mira, and Jax exchanged looks, hearts pounding with triumph tinged by sorrow for Caius's downfall. They knew illusions could always creep back, but for now, they'd done their part.

Homeward Path

In the newly restored clearing, a radiant portal shimmered into view—the gateway leading back to their own world.

Elara placed a guiding hand on Sami's shoulder. "It's time. You've learned what Veritas meant to teach. Go, carry these lessons to your reality."

Sami's throat tightened. "Will we see you again? We might... need more guidance."

Elara smiled softly. "Veritas is always here for those who seek it. And remember—true creation, forged by patience, never truly fades."

Mira felt tears prick her eyes. "Thank you... for everything."

Jax, clearing his throat awkwardly: "I guess... this is goodbye, for now."

Stepping forward, the trio walked into the portal, a swirl of warm light enveloping them. The moment felt like stepping from a dream, but they knew the dream had changed them forever.

Returning to Reality

With a flash, Sami, Mira, and Jax stumbled back into their familiar town—the spot where Skyhaven's glitchy archway had once emerged. Morning sunlight filtered through the real trees. The air smelled of dew and grass. Everything felt sharper, more precious.

Mira, letting out a long breath: "We're... home."

Jax looked around, a relieved grin spreading on his face. "This is definitely it. Real gravity and all."

Sami gazed at his friends, a swirl of emotions raging inside. "We did it, guys... But part of me wonders if Caius might still find a way back."

Mira shrugged, managing a small smile. "If he does, we'll be ready. We've learned too much to let illusions take over again."

Jax nodded, eyes shining. "And maybe... we can help others see that real effort is worth it."

They shared a group hug, the sun rising overhead. Though challenges would always remain, they now carried the enduring strength of Veritas—a testament to the power of *authentic*, patient, collaborative creation.

Mira's Field Note 12
Title: "Back, But Forever Changed"
Observations:

- The swirling illusions collapsed. Caius fled.

- Veritas feels healed, at least for now.

- We returned home and it's comforting to sense solid ground under my feet again.

Personal Realization:

- We once sought easy wins, but discovered that real satisfaction lies in honest struggles.

- Even if illusions come back, we have each other—and we know the difference between temporary perfection and earned success.